The Lost Tale of
GAWAIN

AILSA HOLLAND AND JONATHAN CHADWICK

First published 2013 by MOORMAID PRESS
397 Park Lane, Macclesfield SK11 8JR
www.moormaidpress.co.uk

ISBN 978-0-9927799-0-0

Text © Ailsa Holland 2013
Illustrations © Jonathan Chadwick 2013

All rights reserved. No part of this publication may be reproduced, stored in a retrieval system or transmitted in any form or by any means, electronic, mechanical, photocopying, recording or otherwise, without the prior written permission of the publisher.

Printed and bound by Blurb Inc. www.blurb.co.uk.
The Blurb-provided layout designs and graphic elements are copyright Blurb Inc. This book was created using the Blurb creative publishing service. The book author retains sole copyright to his or her contributions to this book.

Introduction

'The Lost Tale of Gawain' project was intended as both a gentle hoax and also a homage to the exquisite beauty of medieval manuscripts and the engaging simplicity of medieval romance.

Created specially for Macclesfield's Barnaby Festival 2013 Art Trail, the exhibition included six double-spread 'facsimiles' from a 'recently discovered' medieval manuscript and the supposedly medieval book itself in a glass case. In fact the gold-illuminated illustrations, by Jonathan Chadwick, showed scenes from a story, written by Ailsa Holland, of Gawain's adventures in Macclesfield: a sequel to the (genuine) medieval story of *Sir Gawain and the Green Knight*, which is judged from its dialect to have been written in this area.

The exhibition was on show 14-30 June 2013 in St Michael and All Angels Church, Macclesfield.

On 23 June 2013 around 150 people came to listen to a performance of the tale, with Ailsa as storyteller and with live cello music and song by Angela Aiken and Lili Holland-Fricke.

The show returned by popular demand on 2 November 2013, in association with Entropy Events, in St Michael's medieval Savage Chapel, where the intimate atmosphere added to the magic.

Introduction from the exhibition catalogue

The old leather book containing this wonderful story is reported to have been found in the attic of a weaver's cottage in Macclesfield, in an old trunk, whose lock had been rusted up for decades.* How it came to be there is a mystery, one which scholars will undoubtedly spend many hours trying to solve in years and decades to come.

The book contains many important and exciting texts but most of interest for Macclesfield is the story whose illuminated illustrations are exhibited here. It is a 'sequel' to the world-famous tale of *Sir Gawain and the Green Knight* (c.1400), whose dialect suggests that it was written in this area, where the three counties of Derbyshire, Cheshire and Staffordshire meet. Indeed, the magical Green Chapel in the story is widely held to be based on Ludd's Church in Back Forest, Staffordshire.**

This newly discovered 'lost tale' of Gawain makes reference to localities in and around Macclesfield, including: Shutlingsloe, Wildboarclough, Tegg's Nose, Macclesfield Castle and Ludd's Church itself.

It contains many elements and themes commonly found in medieval romance: a quest, tasks, a hunt, magic, a beautiful young woman – and the importance of knightly behaviour. Like *Sir Gawain and the Green Knight*, it has a very unified narrative in comparison with most medieval romances, which generally consist of many unconnected episodes.

The quality and quantity of the exquisite illustrations and wonderfully detailed borders suggest that this was a book commissioned by a very wealthy patron. Make sure you let the gold illuminations catch the light and look out for the poor scribe's complaints in the margins.

Professor R.R. Josephine Neiklot
Moorlands University, June 2013

---

* *Macclesfield Evening News,* 23 June 2012.
** Elliott RWV, 'Landscape and Geography', in *A Companion to the Gawain-Poet* (Brewer D, Gibson J, eds) (DS Brewer; 1997), pp. 105–117.

List of Illustrations

page

Gawain returns to the Green Chapel — 8

Bertilak gives Gawain a letter — 10

A wolf in Macclesfield Forest — 12

The town of Macclesfield — 14

The button-maker — 16

The house of books — 18

Gawain and Ganymede leave Macclesfield — 22

The knights of the Round Table spent each New Year at Camelot, feasting. Gawain was not so merry as the others. He remembered the visit of the Green Knight and how he was tested and disgraced. He felt bound to ride back to the Green Chapel.

But Arthur kept Gawain at court through the winter months, hunting and jousting with his fellow knights. When the snow was gone and the moat was water once again, he gave him leave to go. Arthur was sad but he knew Gawain's heart.

So in spring Gawain prepared his good horse Gringolet for this journey for the fifth time. He took his sword and his pentangle shield and set off.

As he rode through woods and along streams, he saw how life was coming back to the world. Bright green buds burst from the trees; bluebells, sorrel and celandine covered the forest floor and river banks; birds sang in the spring sun.

Bot quen þe hunteȝ hym herd of her dryȝe strokeȝ,
þen, braynwod for bate, on burneȝ he rareȝ,
Hurteȝ hem ful heterly þer he forth hyȝeȝ,
And mony arȝed þerat, and on lyte droȝen.
Bot þe lorde on a lyȝt horce launces hym after,
As burne bolde vpon bent his buȝle he bloweȝ,
He rechated, and rode þurȝ roneȝ ful þyk...

Suande þis wylde swyn til þe sunne schafted.
Þis day wyth þis ilk dede þay dryuen on þis wyse,
Whyle oure luflych lede lys in his bedde,
Gawayn grayþely at home, in gereȝ ful ryche
of hewe.
Þe lady noȝt forȝate,
Com to hym to salue.
Ful erly ho watȝ hym ate
His mode for to remwe.
Ho commes to þe cortyn, and at þe knyȝt totes.
Sir Wawen her welcumed worþy on fyrst,
And ho hym ȝeldeȝ aȝayn ful ȝerne of hir wordeȝ,
Setteȝ hir softly by his syde, and swyþely ho laȝeȝ,
And wyth a luflych loke ho layde hym þyse wordeȝ:
Sir, ȝif ȝe be Wawen, wonder me þynkkeȝ,
Wyȝe þat is so wel wrast alway to god,
And conneȝ not of compaynye þe costeȝ vndertake,
And if mon kennes yow hom to knowe, ȝe kest hom of your mynde.
Þou hatȝ forȝeten ȝederly þat ȝisterday I taȝtte
Bi alder-truest token of talk þat I cowþe.
'What is þat?' quoþ þe wyȝhe, 'Iwysse I wot neuer:
If hit be sothe þat ȝe breue, þe blame is myn awen.'
'ȝet I kende yow of kyssyng,' quoþ þe clere þenne,
Quere-so countenaunce is couþe quikly to clayme;
þat bicumes vche a knyȝt þat cortaysy vses.

Do way,' quoþ þat derf mon, 'my dere, þat speche,
For þat durst I not do, lest I deuayed were.
If I were werned, I were wrang, iwysse, ȝif I profered.'
'Ma fay,' quoþ þe meré wyf,
'Ȝe may not be werned,
Ȝe ar stif innoghe to constrayne wyth strenkþe, ȝif yow lykeȝ,
Ȝif any were so vilanous þat yow denaye wolde.'
'Ȝe, be God,' quoþ Gawayn, 'good is your speche,
Bot þrete is vnþryuande in þede þer I lende,
And vche gift þat is geuen not with goud wylle.
I am at your comaundement, to kysse quen yow lykeȝ,
Ȝe may lach quen yow lyst, and leue quen yow þynkkeȝ,
in space.'
Þe lady loutȝ adoun,
And comly kysses his face,
Much speche þay þer expoun
Of druryes greme and grace.

Nue parchment, bad ink.
I rue nothing more.

The Lost Tale of Gawain

After many days Gawain rode over the Roaches and reached the Back Forest. The crooked trees were like old men with twisted fingers. *Perhaps at night,* thought Gawain, *the forest is full of wizards.*

Each time Gawain sought the Green Chapel he had trouble anew, as though the forest were playing a game with him. There was no path: the greenest of green ferns covered the ground.

After several hours Gawain found the chapel and walked down into it, like walking into a lake. Here it was always cold and damp, be it winter or spring.

Gawain stood between the walls hung with tapestries of moss and for the first time he felt no shame. He heard his own laughter ring like the morning bell. "I will ride and see that Bertilak," he said. "If the Lord will show me the way."

Bi þe bozt al of þe hozes
þe lappeȝ þay lance bihynde.
To hewe hit in two þay hozes,
Bi þe bakbon to vnbynde.
Boþe þe hide and þe halce þay heuen of þenne,
And ryþen vnder þay þe rygge rwnest fro þe chyne.
And þe corbeles fee þay kest in a greue.

þenn þurlez þay aþer þit rize þurz, & þe ryble,
And hengen þenne aþer bi hoʒez of þe fourchez,
Vche frete for his fee, as fallez for to haue.
Upon a felle of þe fayre best fede þay hayre hounder
Wyth þe lyuere and þe lyȝtez, þe leþer of
þe paunchez,
And bred baþed in blod blende þeramongez.
Baldely þay blew prys, barez þayer rachchez,
Syþen folge þay her flesche, folden to home,
Strakande ful stoutly mony stif moetz.
Bi þat þe daylyȝt watz done þe douthe watz
al wonen
Into þe comly castel, þer þe knyȝt biȝez
ful stille,
Wyth blys and bryȝt fyr bette.
þe lorde is comen þertylle,
When Gawayn wyth hym mette
þer watz bot wele at wylle.

Thenne comaunded þe lorde in þat sale to
samen alle þe meny,
Boþe þe ladyes on lofte to lyȝt with her burdez
Bifore alle þe folk on þe flette, frekez he beddez
Verayly his venysoun to fech hym byforne,
And al godly in gomen Gawayn he called,
Techez hym to þe tayles of ful tayt bestez,
Schewez hym þe schyrez greue schorne vpon rybbez.
'How payez yow þis play? haf I prys wonnen?
Haue I þryuandely þonk þurȝ my craft serued?'

'Ȝe iwysse,' quoþ þat oþer wyȝe, 'here is
wayth fayrest
þat I seȝ þis seuen ȝere in sesoun of wynter.'
'And al I gif yow, Gawayn,' quoþ þe gome þenne,
'For by acorde of couenaunt ȝe craue hit as
your awen.'

'þis is soth,' quoþ þe segg, 'I say yow þat ilke:
þat I haf worthyly wonnen þis wonez wythinne,
Iwysse with as god wylle hit worþez to ȝourez.'
He hasppez his fayre hals his armez wythinne,
And kysses hym as comlyly as he couþe awyse.
'Tas yow þer my cheuicaunce, I cheued no more.
I wowche hit saf fynly, þaȝ feler hit were.'
'Hit is god,' quoþ þe godmon, 'grant mercy þerfore.
Hit may be such hit is þe better, and ȝe me
breue wolde
Where ȝe wan þis ilk wele bi wytte of
yorseluen.'
'þat watz not forward,' quoþ he, 'frayst me
no more.
For ȝe haf tan þat yow tydez, traue non oþer
ȝe mowe.'
þay laȝed, and made hem blyþe
Wyth loteȝ þat were to lowe.
To soper þay ȝede as-swyþe,
Wyth dayntes nwe innowe.

He found the hall he sought as evening fell. At the gatehouse he called: "Sir Gawain of Camelot!" and Bertilak himself hurried out to welcome him and bid him be their guest for as long as he should wish.

Gawain stayed for fourteen nights. In the day he hunted with his host. In the evening he sat and feasted and made merry with the ladies, who loved his smile and his courteous ways.

On the fifteenth day Gawain told Bertilak that it was time he returned to Camelot to serve Arthur. Bertilak said he would be sorry to see him go but could not stop his duty to his king.

"But let me ask one favour of you in return for your merriment here. Would you take a letter to the lord of the castle at Macclesfield? It is a delicate matter. But I know I can trust a knight of the Round Table."

And vvhen by þe chymnes, in chamber þay seten,
Wyȝes þe walle vvyn vveȝed to hem oft,
And eft in her bourdyng þay baþen in þe morn
To fille þe same forvvardeȝ þat þay byfore maden:
Wat chaunce so bytydeȝ hor chevysaunce to chaunge,
What nevveȝ so þay nome, at naȝt qven þay meten,
Þay acorded of þe covenaunteȝ byfore þe court alle.

Þe bugle vvatȝ breþt forth in bonde at þat tyme,
Þenne þay louveloch lysten leve at þe last,
Veche burne to hir bedde busked bylyve.
Bi þat þe coke hade crovven and calleþ bot þryse,
Þe lorde vvatȝ lopen of hir bedde, þe leudeȝ vchone.
So þat þe mete and þe masse vvatȝ metely delyvered,
Þe douthe dressed to þe vvod, er any day sprenged,
to chace.
Heȝ with hunte and horneȝ
Þurȝ playneȝ þay passe in space,
Vncoupleȝ among þo horneȝ
Racheȝ þat ran on race.

Sone þay calle of a quert in a ker syde,
Þe hunt rehayted þe houndeȝ þat hit fyrst moneged,
Wylde wordeȝ hym vvarp vvyth a vvrast noyce.
Þe houndeȝ þat hit herde hastid þider svvyþe,
And fellen as fast to þe fyut, fourty at oneȝ.

Such a glaver ande glam of gedered racheȝ
Ros, þat þe rocheres rungen aboute.
Hunteres hem hardened with horne and vvyth mvthe,
Þen al in a semblyde svveyed togeder,
Bitvvene a florche in þat froth and a foo cragge;
In a knot bi a clyffe, at þe kerre syde,
Þer as þe rogh rocher vnrydely vvatȝ fallen,
Þay ferden to þe fyndyng, and freke hem after.

Þay vmbekesten þe knarre and þe knot boþe,
Wyȝeȝ, vvhyl þay vvysten vvel vvyþinne
Hem hit vvere,
Þe best þat þer breved vvatȝ vvyth þe blodhoundeȝ.
Þenne þay beten on þe busker, and bede hym vp ryse,
And he vnsoundyly out soȝt segges ouerþvvert;
On þe sellokest svvyn svvenged out þere,
Long sythen fro þe sounder þat syȝed for olde,
For he vvatȝ breme, bor alþer-grattest,
Ful grymme quen he gronyed; þenne greved mony,
For þre at þe fyrst þrast he þryȝt to þe erþe,
And sparred forth good sped boute spyt more.
Þise oþer halovved hyghe! ful hyȝe, and hay!
hay! cryed,
Haden horneȝ to mouþe, heterly rechated;
Mony vvatȝ þe myry mouthe of men and of houndeȝ
Þat buskkeȝ after þir bor vvith bost and
vvyth noyse to quelle.
Ful oft he bydeȝ þe baye,
And maymeȝ þe mute inn melle,
He hurteȝ of þe houndeȝ, and þay
Ful ȝomerly ȝaule and ȝelle.

Schalteȝ to schos at hym schoven to þenne,
Haled to hym of her arvveȝ, hitten hym oft;
Bot þe poynteȝ payred at þe pyth þat pyȝt in his scheldeȝ,
And þe barbeȝ of his browe bite non vvolde,
Þaȝ þe schaven schaft schyvered in peceȝ,
Þe hede hypped aȝayn vvere-so-euer hit hitte.

Gawain could not refuse. He put the letter, with its seal of green wax, into the pocket of his saddle. The ladies wept and threw flowers in his path as he made his way out of the courtyard and through the gatehouse to find the town called Macclesfield.

He rode up hill and down dale. At an inn with the sign of the wild boar he took bread and meat and ale, then rode on, up to a windswept top from which he could see all the world for miles around – woods and rocky edges and a plain, wide as the sea.

He rode down into a forest of ash, rowan, beech and hornbeam. In a clearing he heard a low growl behind him and turned to see a huge black wolf with eyes of azurite blue.

Gawain was not afraid. He had fought many animals and monsters. He drew his sword but as he raised his arm to strike he heard a woman's voice: "Spare him!" He waved the weapon away and the wolf fled into the darkness of the trees.

Gawain looked round to see who had spoken but only saw a figure in a blue hooded cloak, running away into the forest. He followed her as fast as he could but failed to find her.

Þenne ho gef hym god day, and wyth a glent laȝed
And as ho stod, ho stonyed hym wyth ful stor wordez:
'Now he þat spedez vche spech þis disport ȝelde yow!
Bot þat ȝe be Gawan, hit gotz in mynde.'
'Quer-fore?' quoþ þe freke, and freschly he askez,
Ferde lest he hade fayled in fourme of his castes:
Bot þe burde hym blessed, and 'Bi þis skyl' sayde.

So god as Gawayn gaynly is halden,
And cortaysye is closed so clene in hymseluen,
Couth not lyȝtly haf lenged so long wyth a lady,
Bot he has craued a cosse, bi his courtaysye,
Bi sum towch of summe tryfle at sum talez ende.'
Þen quoþ Wowen: 'I-wysse, worþe as yow lykez;
I schal kysse at your comaundment, as a knyȝt fallez,

And fire, lest he displease yow, so plede hit no more.'
Ho comes nerre with þat, and cachez hym in armez,
Loutez luflych adoun and þe leude kyssez.
Þay comly bykennen to Kryst ayþer oþer:
Ho dos hir forth at þe dore withouten dyn more.
And he rycher hym to ryse and rapes hym sone,
Clepes to his chamberlayn, choses his wede,
Boȝez forth, quen he watz boun, blyþely to masse.
And þenne he meued to his mete þat menskly hym keped,
And made myry al day, til þe mone rysed,
with game.
Watz neuer freke fayrer fonge
Bitwene two so dyngne dame,
þe alder and þe ȝonge.
Much solace set þay same.

And ay þe lorde of þe londe is lent on his gamnez,
To hunt in holtez and heþe at hyndez barayne;
Such a sowme he þer slowe bi þat þe sunne heldet,
Of dos and of oþer dere, to deme were wonder.
Þenne ferdly þay flokked in folk at þe laste,
And quykly of þe quelled dere a querre þay maken.
Þe best boȝed þerto with burnez innoghe,
Gederes þe grattest of gres þat þer were,
And didden hym derely vndo as þe dede askez;
Serched hem at þe asay summe þat þer were,
Two fyngeres þay fonde of þe fowlest of alle.
Syþen þay slyt þe slot, sesed þe erber,
Schaued wyth a scharp knyf, and þe schyre knitten;
Syþen rytte þay þe foure lymmes, and rent of þe hyde,
Þen brek þay þe balé, þe bowelez out token
Lystily for laucyng þe lere of þe knot:
Þay gryped to þe gargulun, and grayþely departed
Þe wesaunt fro þe wynt-hole, and walt out þe gutteȝ;
Þen scher þay out þe schulderez with her scharp knyuez,
Haled hem by a lyttel hole to haue hole sydez.
Siþen britned þay þe brest and brayden hit in twynne,
And eft at þe gargulun bigynez on þenne,
Ryuez hit vp radly ryȝt to þe byȝt,
Voydez out þe avanters, and verayly þerafter
Alle þe rymez by þe rybbez radly þay lancen.
So ryde þay of by resoun bi þe rygge bonez,
Euenden to þe haunche, þat henged alle samen,
And heuen hit vp al hole, and hewen hit of þere,
And þat þay neme for þe noumbles bi nome,
as I trowe, bi kynde;

Bi þe, my hand

Gawain rode out of the woods through fields and meadows, until he saw the town on top of a small hill, with its castle and its church. He crossed the ford of the river called Bollin then rode up a street of cobblestones towards the castle.

A young woman sat outside a cottage in the sun and sang; and all the while her small deft fingers wound thread around a piece of wood. The thread shone in the sunlight and the song was as fine as a blackbird's and Gawain could only sit in his saddle and stare, like a deer who has spotted his hunter.

The young woman knotted the thread and stopped her song and spoke to Gawain.

"Would you like to buy buttons, Sir Knight? Scarlet buttons for your tunic? Or purple for your lady?"

"I have no lady," said Gawain, and his face was the palest red. "I am bound for the castle."

The young woman bowed her head and took up her thread and began a new song.

Ful erly bifore þe day þe folk vprysen,
Gestes þat go wolde hor gromez þay calden,
And þay busken vp bilyue blonkkez to sadel,
Tyffen her takles, trussen her males,
Richen hem þe rychest, to ryde alle arayde,
Lepen vp lyʒtly, lachen her brydeles,
Vche wyʒe on his way þer hym wel lyked.

þe leue lorde of þe londe watz not þe last
Arayed for þe rydyng, with renkkez ful mony;
Ete a sop hastyly, when he hade herde masse,
With bugle to bent-felde he buskez bylyue.
By þat any daylyʒt lemed vpon erþe
He with his haþeles on hyʒe horsses weren.
þenne þise cacheres þat couþe cowpled hor houndez,
Vnclosed þe kenel dore and calde hem þeroute,
Blwe bygly in buglez þre bare mote;
Braches bayed þerfore and breme noyse maked;
And þay chastysed and charred on chasyng þat went,
A hundreth of hunteres, as I haf herde telle,
of þe best.
To trystors vewters ʒod,
Couples hunter of kest;
þer rurd in þat forest
At þe fyrst quethe of þe quest quakede þe wylde.
Der drof in þe dale, doted for drede,
Hiʒed to þe hyʒe, bot heterly þay were
Restayed with þe stablye, þat stoutly ascryed.
þay let þe hertez haf þe gate, with þe hyʒe hedes,
þe breme bukkez also with hor brode paumez;
For þe fre lorde hade defende in fermysoun tyme
þat þer schulde no mon meue to þe male dere.
þe hindez were halden in with hay! and war!
þe does dryuen with gret dyn to þe depe slades;
þer myʒt mon se, as þay slypte, slentyng

of arwes—
At vche wende vnder wande wapped a flone—
þat bigly bote on þe broun with ful brode hedez.
What! þay brayen, and bleden, bi bonkkez þay deʒen,
And ay rachches in a res radly hem folʒes,
Hunteres wyth hyʒe horne hasted hem after
Wyth such a crakkande kry as klyffes haden brusten.
What wylde so atwaped wyʒes þat schotten
Watz al toraced and rent at þe resayt,
Bi þay were tened at þe hyʒe and taysed to þe wattrez;
þe ledez were so lerned at þe loʒe trysteres,
And þe grehoundez so grete, þat geten hem bylyue
And hem to-flosches, as fast as freke myʒt loke, þer ryʒt.
þe lorde for blys abloy
Ful oft con launce and lyʒt,
And drof þat day wyth joy
Thus to þe derk nyʒt.

þus laykez þis lorde by lynde-wodez euez,
And Gawayn þe god mon in gay bed lygez,
Lurkkez quyl þe daylyʒt lemed on þe wowes,
Vnder couertour ful clere, cortyned aboute;
And as in slomeryng he slode, sleʒly he herde
A littel dyn at his dor, and derfly vpon;

Gawain rode up to the castle gate and hit on the door with the hilt of his sword. "I am Sir Gawain of Camelot. I bring a letter from Bertilak." The great gate was opened. The castle lord – his name was Jauderel – met Gawain in the courtyard. Gawain held out the letter with Bertilak's green seal but the lord just laughed. "So you are the latest knight to take on my challenge."

Now Gawain, as you know, knew nothing of a challenge, but he was a knight of great courtesy and chivalry. He could not refuse to take on the task even for one as two-faced as Bertilak. The lord told him of three tests. "If you fail just one test you will not return to Camelot but remain in my service in Macclesfield as so many before you."

The worthy knight said, "I am ready."

First he had to hew seven blocks of ivory-coloured stone from a quarry on a hill. This was work to break all backs but Gawain made no complaint and the blocks were brought to the castle within one day. For the second task he had to ride into the forest and bring back a stag with white marks on its flanks. This was the hardest hunt of Gawain's life for the stag was strong and fast but by evening the head with its splendid antlers was delivered to the castle hall.

And he heuez vp his hed out of þe cloþes,
A corner of þe cortyn he cazt vp a lyttel,
And waytez warly þiderwarde quat hit be myzt.
Hit watz þe ladi, loflyest to beholde,
Þat droz þe dor after hir ful dernly and stille,
And bozed towarde þe bed: and þe burne schamed,
And layde hym doun lyztyly, and let as he slepte.

And ho steppes stilly and stel to his bedde,
Kest vp þe cortyn and creped withinne,
And set hir ful softly on þe bed-syde,
And lenged þere selly longe to loke quen he wakened.
Þe lede lay lurked a ful longe quyle,
Compast in his concience to quat þat cace myzt
Meue oþer amount—to meruayle hym þozt,
Bot zet he sayde in hymself, 'More semly hit were
To aspye wyth my spelle in space quat ho wolde.'
Þen he wakenede, and wroth, and to hir warde torned,
And vnlouked his yze-lyddez, and let as hym wondered,
And sayned hym, as bi his saze þe sauer to worthe, with hande.

Wyth chynne and cheke ful swete,
Boþe quit and red in blande,
Ful lufly con ho lete
Wyth lyppez smal lazande.

'God moroun, Sir Gawayn,' sayde þat gay lady,
'Ze ar a sleper vnslyze, þat mon may slyde hider.
Now ar ze tan as-tyt! Bot true vus may schape,
I schal bynde yow in your bedde, þat be ze trayst':
Al lazande þe lady lanced þo bourdez.
'Goud moroun, gay,' quoþ Gawayn þe blyþe,
'Me schal worþe at your wille, and þat me wel lykez,
For I zelde me zederly, and zeze after grace,
And þat is þe best, be my dome, for me byhouez nede':

And þus he bourded azayn with mony a blyþe lazter.
'Bot wolde ze, lady louely, þen leue me grante,
And deprece your prysoun, and pray hym to ryse,
I wolde boze of þis bed, and busk me better,
I schulde keuer þe more comfort to karp yow wyth.'
'Nay for soþe, beau sir,' sayd þat swete,
'Ze schal not rise of your bedde, I rych yow better,
I schal happe yow here þat oþer half als,
And syþen karp wyth my knyzt þat I kazt haue.
For I wene wel, iwysse, Sir Wowen ze ar,
Þat alle þe worlde worchipez quere-so ze ride.
Your honour, your hendelayk is hendely praysed
With lordez, wyth laydez, with alle þat lyf ber.
And now ze ar here, iwysse, and we bot oure one,
My lorde and his ledez ar on lenþe faren,
Oþer burnez in her bedde, and my burdez als,
Þe dor drawen and dit with a derf haspe,
And syþen I haue in þis hous hym þat al lykez,
I schal ware my whyle wel, quyl hit lastez,
with tale.
Ze ar welcum to my cors,
Yowre awen won to wale,
Me behouez of fyne force
Your seruaunt be, and schale.'

This is sad! O little Book! A day will come in truth
when someone over your page will run the hand that wrote
it is no more...

The lord said, "I commend you, knight of Camelot, but there is one test left. From the castle cellars lead tunnels that travel under the town. Find the tunnel to the house of books and complete the task that is set you."

At the tunnel's mouth Gawain took a burning torch and walked into the dark. The ways were many and woven like a spider's web but at each junction Gawain scratched a mark on the wall with a stone from the quarry. He found the entrance to an inn, a butcher's store and a reeking dungeon. His torch was all but spent when he saw some steps leading to a trap door.

He climbed through to a room whose walls seemed made of books. There was no-one there and no other door than the way he had come. Brave as he was, Gawain got a fright when the wall in front of him began to shift and turn and from behind the books came an old man in a long golden robe. He smiled.

"You are welcome, Sir Gawain. Here is your riddle: What weighs no more than a feather but is stronger than a man? You may ask counsel of one person as you try to solve the riddle. Choose wisely for this is a task that most knights fail. Give the lord Jauderel your answer by nightfall."

Gawain thanked the old man and left the house by the street door and walked back up the hill towards the castle. He was sombre in his thoughts and felt alone in this strange town. Whom could he ask for counsel? He longed for Camelot, his wise king, and the knights who were his brothers. Here he only knew Bertilak who had twice betrayed him.

Then, he saw the church and an anchorite's tower. Surely, no one could be wiser than an anchorite. Gawain's heart lifted. But just as he reached the tower he heard once again the song of the button-maker from the street below. He thought he would rest awhile and listen to the melody. And he walked towards the music as though pulled by a thread he could not see.

The young woman looked up from her work. She smiled to see Gawain. "Can I help you, Sir Knight?" she asked. And she was so fair that Gawain told her of the riddle. And then she laughed, and picked up a red thread from her lap, and gave it to Gawain and bid him break it. He took it from her and held it between his hands but pull as he might the thread did not snap. He looked at her in wonder. "Is this sorcery?" he asked.

"No, Sir Knight, it is silk," was her reply. "And it is your answer."

Gawain was astonished. "And why have so many knights failed this task?" "Because you, gentle Gawain, are the first to choose me as your adviser."

Gawain ran to the castle and gave his answer to the lord Jauderel who sat in the Great Hall. The lord said, "Gawain, you are the strongest and wisest of knights. But I will keep my word and set you free to ride again to Camelot and your king."

Gawain was filled with joy and took Gringolet from the Castle stables and led him through the gate. But he did not mount his steed and head back to Arthur's court. He walked down to the button-maker and asked her name and would she be his wife. She said her name was Freda and yes, with all her heart, if they could stay in Macclesfield. And in his love and courtesy he could not refuse her.

The next time that the bright green buds came back to the trees and the bluebells began to flower, Gawain's wife brought a child into the world, a boy. They called him Ganymede. He was a child like the sun. And Gawain was knight and husband and father and each day he loved his wife and son more.

Another year passed and as spring became summer Freda's mood grew dark. One day she spoke to Gawain.

'In god fayth,' quoþ Gawayn, 'gayn hit me þynkkeȝ,
þaȝ I be not now he þat ȝe of speken;
To reche to such reuerence as ȝe reherce here
I am wyȝe vnworþy, I wot wel myseluen.
Bi God, I were glad, and yow god þoȝt,
At saȝe oþer at seruyce þat I sette myȝt
To þe plesaunce of your prys—hit were a pure ioye.'

'In god fayth, Sir Gawayn,' quoþ þe gay lady,
'þe prys and þe prowes þat pleseȝ al oþer,
If I hit lakked oþer set at lyȝt, hit were
littel daynté;
Bot hit ar ladyes innoȝe þat leuer wer nowþe
Haf þe, hende, in hor holde, as I þe habbe here,
To daly with derely your daynté wordeȝ,
Keuer hem comfort and colen her careȝ,
þen much of þe garysoun oþer golde þat þay hauen.
Bot I louue þat ilk lorde þat þe lyfte haldeȝ,
I haf hit holly in my honde þat al desyres,
þurȝ grace.'
Scho made hym so gret chere,
þat watȝ so fayr of face,
þe knyȝt with speches skere
Answared to vche a cace.

'Madame,' quoþ þe myry mon, 'Mary yow ȝelde,
For I haf founden, in god fayth, yowre
fraunchis nobele,
And oþer ful much of oþer folk fongen bi hor dedeȝ,
Bot þe daynté þat þay delen, for my
disert nys euen,
Hit is þe worchyp of yourself, þat noȝt
bot wel conneȝ.'
'Bi Mary,' quoþ þe menskful, 'me þynk
hit an oþer;
For were I worth al þe wone of wymmen alyue,
And al þe wele of þe worlde were in my honde,
And I schulde chepen and chose to cheue me a lorde,

For þe costes þat I haf knowen vpon þe,
knyȝt, here,
Of bewté, and debonerté, and blyþe semblaunt,
And þat I haf er herkkened and halde hit
here trwee,
Þer schulde no freke vpon folde bifore yow be chosen.'
'Iwysse, worþy,' quoþ þe wyȝe, 'ȝe haf
waled wel better,
Bot I am proude of þe prys þat ȝe put on me,
And, soberly your seruaunt, my souerayn
I holde yow,

And yowre knyȝt I becom,
and Kryst yow forȝelde.'
Þus þay meled of muchquat til mydmorn paste,
And ay þe lady let lyk as hym loued mych;
Þe freke ferde with defence, and feted ful fayre—
'þaȝ I were burde bryȝtest,' þe burde in
mynde hade.
þe lasse luf in his lode for lur þat he soȝt
boute hone,
þe dunte þat schulde hym deue,
And nedeȝ hit most be done.
þe lady þenn spek of leue,
He granted hir ful sone.

"It is time for you to leave Macclesfield. Our son should be raised as a knight at Arthur's court." This had been in Gawain's heart since his child was born and so he kissed his wife and promised that she would be happy in Camelot.

"No," she said. "I will not come with you. I must stay here and protect my brother. Morgan le Fay has a feud with my father, the keeper of the books, and she has magicked my brother into a wolf. I would fear for his life if I were to go away."

And Gawain knew then that his wife was the woman from the forest who had stayed his sword. "Yes," she said with a smile. "I saw then how good and courteous a man you were and our son will be the same. And in Camelot, with the help of the great sorcerer Merlin, he will be safe from Morgan le Fay." Gawain begged his wife to go away with them. "I will fight this Morgan le Fay and your brother will be free." But she was quite firm and would not be moved.

So at night on the feast of St Barnabas Gawain mounted his horse and with Freda's help he bound his child to sit in front of him with a scarlet cloth. And Gawain kissed his wife's lips and she kissed his eyes, and as he rode away he wept and she wept, and the blue of her silk cloak shone dark in the moonlight.

When the Nightingale Sings
(The Button-Maker's Song)

When the nyhtegale singes,
    The wodes waxen grene,
Lef ant gras ant blosme springes
    In Averyl, Y wene;
Ant love is to myn herte gon
    With one spere so kene,
Nyht ant day my blod hit drynkes
    Myn herte deth me tene.

Ich have loved al this yer
    That Y may love na more;
Ich have siked moni syk,
    Lemmon, for thin ore,
Me nis love neuer the ner,
    Ant that me reweth sore;
Suete lemmon, thench on me,
    Ich have loved the yore.

When the nightingale sings,
    The woods grow green,
Leaf and grass and blossom spring,
    In April, this I know;
And love has gone at my heart
    With a spear so keen, that
Night and day it drains my blood
    And wounds my heart to death.

All this past year I have loved thee,
    Such that I may love no more.
I have sighed many a sigh,
    Beloved, for thy pity.
My love is never nearer to thee,
    And that grieves me painfully.
Sweet loved one, think on me:
    I have loved thee long.

From the Harley MS 2253 (British Library),
written c. 1310